I0631431

THE BEATINEST* BOY

*Beatinest — surpassing all others, most unusual.

Webster

THE BEATINEST BOY

JESSE STUART

EDITED BY

JIM WAYNE MILLER
JERRY A. HERNDON
JAMES M. GIFFORD

ORIGINAL ILLUSTRATIONS
BY ROBERT HENNEBERGER
BOOK DESIGN
BY ROCKY ZORNES

THE JESSE STUART FOUNDATION

Dedicated to
Kentucky's Teachers

---

*"I am firm in my belief that a teacher
lives on and on through his students.
Good teaching is forever and the
teacher is immortal."*

-Jesse Stuart

The Beatinest Boy
Copyright© 1952 The Curtis Publishing Company
Copyright© 1980 The Jesse Stuart Foundation

All rights reserved. No part of this book may be
reproduced or utilized in any form or by any means,
electronic or mechanical, including photocopying, recording,
or by any information storage or retrieval system, without
permission in writing from the publisher.

Published by:
The Jesse Stuart Foundation
P.O. Box 391 Ashland, KY 41114
1994

FOREWORD

For the seventh year, the Kentucky Jaycees and the Jesse Stuart Foundation are distributing copies of a Jesse Stuart book to sixth graders throughout the state. The purpose of the 1994 Jesse Stuart Book Project is to put a copy of <u>The Beatinest Boy</u> in the hands of as many Kentucky sixth graders as possible, in the hope that the story will encourage them to read for pleasure and thus strengthen their reading skills. It also will promote interest in Kentucky history and literature.

Jesse Stuart once remarked that "If the United States can be called a body, Kentucky can be called its heart." He was speaking metaphorically, of course. But the Jaycees' work on the Jesse Stuart Book Project certainly adds another dimension to the word "heart," and also exemplifies Stuart's own statement, "No joy runs deeper than the feeling that I have helped a youth stand on his own two feet, to have courage and self-reliance and to find himself when he did not know who he was or where he was going."

If you would like to contribute to the Jesse Stuart Book Project, please send your check to The Jesse Stuart Foundation, P. O. Box 391, Ashland, Kentucky 41114. Every $1.50 that you contribute places a much-needed book in the hands of a Kentucky child.

Ms. Judy B. Thomas
Chairperson, Jesse Stuart Foundation

CONTENTS

THE CRY ON THE MOUNTAIN

David took long steps as he walked down the winding path through the cow pasture. He had told his Grandma Beverley that he was going to climb this mountain, go up to the top, and stick his hand through a cloud. Grandma had said that she was too tired to go with him and wanted to go to bed early. Maybe she just wanted to let me go alone, David thought.

David was sure his Grandma Beverley was the smartest, most wonderful woman in the world. She could do just about anything. Ever since his father and mother had died and he'd come to live with her, she had been teaching him wonderful things. He hadn't liked the idea of going to live with the tall, strange woman, but he and she were a real family now. She had shown him how to hunt, how to keep chickens and milk the cow, how to plant potatoes and corn, and how to use a long-handled gooseneck hoe.

Grandma must have felt that he was a great help to her — in fact, didn't she often say he was "the beatinest boy in the world" and claim she couldn't get along without him? Grandma never fussed and she knew an

9

awful lot of useful things.

David climbed higher and higher. He looked through the thin mist above him and he could see the setting sun. Then he put his hand up through the mist and felt the warm rays of the sun. "My hand is through the cloud!" he shouted.

Then he took a few more steps, and he was standing above an endless sea of clouds that covered the whole valley, looking down on them. They were as white as snow and as level as the floor in Grandma Beverley's house. There was a path of golden light streaming across the white cloud floor from the setting sun, and David thought: This is the prettiest thing I have ever seen. I wish Grandma could see this.

While I'm here, I'll look around, David thought, as he walked a little further along the fox hunters' path. He stopped again to look at the sea of clouds around his island. Then he thought he heard a sound.

David put his hand behind his ear and listened. He thought he heard a foxhound whining very faintly. He took in his breath more slowly so that he could hear better. It *is* the sound of a dog! he thought. It's that way! Then he took a few steps in the direction of the sound. He waited again and held his breath so he could listen. It is a dog, he thought. I know it's a dog. It's out on the ridge. Then David ran a few steps in the direction of the sound.

"Here doggy, here doggy!" he called.

But the dog didn't answer him. Then David stood there holding his breath, waiting to hear the dog whine again.

But it didn't, so he walked on until he came to a big log. He sat down on the log to listen for the sound again. In every direction he looked, there were white clouds. The sun had gone down through the clouds, and he felt very lonely upon his island of green with the clouds around him in all directions.

He's not going to whine again, David thought. It was a foxhound down under the mountain. He'd been tracking a fox and he's gone. I'll have to go too, he thought. I'll have to go before it gets too dark. I'm not afraid of the dark, but Grandma warned me not to get lost.

Then he heard the dog's whine again. The sound came from beneath him!

It can't be! David thought, jumping up. Where is it?

"Here doggy, here doggy!" he called.

Then he waited, but there was no answer.

Surely it couldn't be in this log, he thought. Then he ran to one end of the log to see if it were hollow. He looked, but there wasn't any hollow place for a dog to get inside. To be sure, he got down on his knees and felt of the log with his hands. Then he jumped up and ran around to the other end of the log.

"Yes, it is hollow here!" he shouted.

He reached down and took hold of a piece of log, and to his surprise it was rotten. He pulled the piece of log up with his hands. Then he broke off another piece and another. "Dry leaves," he said. He put his hand down on the leaves. "The leaves are warm! Something's been sleeping on 'em!" he shouted. "That dog has just left its bed. It's gone back farther into the log!"

David quickly broke off piece after piece of the rotted log. He followed the big hollow until it ended. And there, crouched back as far as it could get, was a trembling little pup. It whined and shook with fear as David put his hands slowly down to touch it.

"Something told me to climb above this cloud!" David shouted with joy. "I don't know what it was, but I've found me a puppy!"

David lifted the skinny puppy from the log.

"I'm not going to hurt you," he said softly. "You're nearly starved to death. I'll take you home and feed you. Are you sick? What happened that you've lost your hair?"

The puppy's skin was red, and in two places it was bleeding. "Don't be afraid, puppy," David said. "I've got you now. I'll do all I can for you. Grandma and I will help you to get well."

It was a wild little puppy, and it tried to get away from David. But it was too weak to do it. David held it in his arms as he started running back down the path. "I'm taking you home, puppy," he said. "I'll give you sweet milk tonight. Daisy gives milk for Grandma and me and some for Charlie the pig, and she'll give milk for you, too."

As he went down into the cloud mist, he held the puppy closer for fear it would get away and he wouldn't be able to find it. "Who left you up on this mountain, puppy? Did the fox hunters do it? Why did they do it? Was it because you don't have hair on your body? You're an orphan like I was. But Grandma took me and bought me clothes. Maybe Grandma can make the hair grow back on you, little orphan puppy. Grandma can do almost anything."

Before David had reached the valley, he was calling the hungry puppy "Orphan."

GRANDMA TO THE RESCUE

"Grandma, Grandma, wake up and see what I've got!" David called, as he pounded on his grandmother's bedroom door.

"Grandma, Grandma, wake up and see what I've got!"

"Just a minute!" she said, turning over in bed.

Grandma found the matchbox on the chair she kept beside her bed. She struck a match and lighted the kerosene lamp.

"Now, come in and show me!" she said.

David opened her door and rushed into the room with the little puppy in his arms.

"What is it, David?" she asked, straining her eyes at the squirming object. "What color is it?"

"Get your specs on so you can see!" David said.

Grandma reached down to the chair beside her bed and got her glasses. She rubbed her sleepy eyes and put them on.

"Bring it closer so I can see," she said.

David walked up beside the bed and held the puppy in his hands.

"It's a little hound, David," she said, patting its

14

forehead with her wrinkled hand. "But the poor little thing is nearly eaten up with the mange. He's lost his hair, and he's nearly starved to death. Where on earth did you find him?"

"I found him above the clouds in a hollow log," he said proudly. "You know, something told me to go up there tonight. Gee, Grandma, I wish you could have gone with me. The sun was shining on the clouds up there, and it was the prettiest place I have ever seen. I was watching the sunlight on the clouds when I heard a dog whine. Then I went toward the sound, but I couldn't find the dog. Grandma, I sat down on the very log I found Orphan in! I was as still as a mouse and then I heard him whine in the log. I was lucky to find him!"

"Have you named him 'Orphan'?"

"Yes, Grandma. Somebody went away and left him on that high ridge," David said. "I think it must have been a fox hunter who left him. He doesn't have a mother and father and I don't, either. I was an orphan until you took me in. He's an orphan, too! That's why I named him what I did."

"I'll bet he's a fine-blooded hound puppy, David," Grandma said. "Somebody left him to die of the mange. That's why you found him there."

"Can we save him, Grandma?"

"Maybe we can," she said. "He needs warm sweet milk first. Then we'll get Boliver Tussie to help us cure him of the mange. Boliver is the best hound-dog doctor in the valley."

"Gee, I hope we can save him, Grandma," David said,

15

holding the puppy close.

"You go build a fire in the stove while I get up and dress," she said. "We'll warm the milk for him. He doesn't look like he's eaten for days!"

"All right, Grandma."

David went into the kitchen. He put Orphan down on the floor while he laid a handful of kindling in the firebox. Then he struck a match and held it to the kindling. As the little flame leaped up and licked into the dry kindling, David laid sticks of stovewood carefully on the fire. When Grandma dressed and came into the kitchen, the fire was burning and the stove was getting hot.

"Go out to the cellar, David, and fetch me a crock of milk," she said.

David ran out of the kitchen and soon returned with the crock. Grandma Beverley took a long-handled spoon and stirred the cream that had risen to the top. Then she poured a pint of milk into a pan and set it on top of the stove.

"Grandma, do you reckon we can save Orphan?" David asked.

"I don't know, David," she told him. "That mange has a good hold on him. When a dog loses his hair, he might be beyond saving. But we'll do our best."

"I hope we can save him, Grandma."

The skinny hound whined weakly in David's arms.

"He got cold up there on that high ridge without any hair on his body," Grandma Beverley said. "That's why he found a hollow log and crawled into it. I'll bet the poor thing almost froze to death up there."

16

Grandma put her finger into the milk to see if it was warm enough.

"He wouldn't have lived much longer if I hadn't found him tonight, would he, Grandma?"

"I'm afraid not," she said. "Let's see if he's too far gone to eat."

Grandma set the pan of milk down on the floor, and David got down on his knees beside it. He put Orphan down close to the pan.

"Put his nose close to the milk, David," she said. "Let him smell it."

David pushed Orphan's nose down into the milk. The puppy licked out his little red tongue to taste it, then began to lap it up greedily.

"Oh, Grandma, he's eating! He's eating!" David shouted.

"He'll feel better after he eats," she said. "Look how raw his skin is!"

"He's bleeding in two or three places, Grandma!"

Orphan drank all the milk there was in the pan.

"Grandma, he needs more," David said.

"That's enough for him tonight," she said. "We mustn't give him enough to founder him. Fix him a bed. In the morning we'll go see Boliver!"

"Can't we go tonight, Grandma?"

"No, Boliver will be in bed."

"Then we'll get up early in the morning," David said.

"You'll have to go to bed and get some sleep. And little Orphan will have to get some sleep too, after drinking all that milk," Grandma answered.

"Grandma, can I let him sleep upstairs in my room tonight?" David asked.

"Yes, if you'll make him a bed down on the floor," she said. "Don't put him in the bed with you. We will try to get him well again so hair will grow over his body, and he'll be a pretty hound puppy."

"All right, Grandma, I'll make him a bed on the floor under my bed," David said, as he started climbing the steep stairs to his room. "In the morning we'll take him to Boliver Tussie's, won't we?"

"That's right, David," she said, smiling, as she watched the boy climb the stairs with Orphan.

18

DR. BOLIVER TUSSIE

"Poor little thing," Grandma Beverley said, looking down into her apron. "He's scratched himself with his toenails until he's bleeding again. The poor little thing was left on that ridge to die, and you found him, David!"

David looked up at his grandmother.

"Grandma, do you reckon Boliver Tussie can save him?" he asked.

"I don't know, David. But if anybody in the valley can save him, it will be Boliver!"

Grandma Beverley's long dress dragged over the dew-covered grass along the path. She had always lifted her skirt above the dewy weeds when she went to Blakesburg with David. But she couldn't, now, for she was holding Orphan's scratchy, itching body in her apron.

When Grandma and David followed the path around a high rock cliff, they came to Boliver Tussie's log cabin.

"You knock on the door, David," said his grandmother. "Boliver might not be up yet. I don't see any smoke from the chimney. They never get up as early as we do."

David stepped up on a little porch that didn't have

19

a roof over it. He knocked on the door and waited. No one came, so he knocked again. As he knocked a third time, the door suddenly opened, and there stood the strangest looking man David had ever seen.

"What do you want, Sonny?" asked the tall, red-faced man. He spoke in a soft voice that was just above a whisper. "I-doggies, you got me outten the bed. Must be something wrong someplace. That's when they come and get me outten the bed and I don't get my mornin' nap!"

Boliver Tussie laughed at his own words. His laugh was a wild, screaming laugh like the foxhounds' barking David had heard when the hounds chased the fox across his grandmother's farm. Boliver Tussie stood before him, barefooted, wearing only a pair of overalls with suspenders across his bare shoulders. There was a thin red beard on his face that hung from his chin in a long point. The bright red hair on his head came nearly to his shoulders. He had long arms and thin hands that dangled almost to his knees.

"Yes, there is something wrong," David said, with a sob. "I've found a puppy, and it's nearly dead from the mange. Grandma says you might be able to save him. Can you?"

"Oh, I didn't see Cynthia out there!" Boliver said, rubbing his eyes and yawning. "Say, we'll do something about that puppy, specially if he's a hound! Let me see 'im!"

Grandma Beverley stepped up on the porch without saying a word.

20

"Don't tell me you're interested in saving a hound, Cynthia!" Boliver said. "After all the eggs my hounds have got from your hens' nests, I'd think you'd hate a hound!"

"But Boliver, David loves the little thing," Grandma Beverley said, "and I do, too! I can't stand to see a hound suffer!"

She opened her apron so Boliver could see the bleeding puppy.

"Poor little thing," Boliver said, lifting the whining puppy from the apron and fondling him with soft caresses. "Where did ye get 'im? He's a hound, all right! Who'd be low-down enough to treat a young hound like this?"

"I found him on the high ridge where the fox hunters build their fires," David said. "I found him in a hollow log where he'd crawled to die!"

"I-doggies, I'll put a curse on the heathen who left 'im there," Boliver said. "I can put the curse on any man who mistreats a hound!"

When David looked away from the porch, he counted seven fine-looking hounds of various sizes and colors. They were well-fed and happy. They lifted their tails up proudly in one and two curls. When David turned to look at Boliver again, three red-headed boys, all smaller than he was, were standing beside Boliver in the door. They were barefooted and wore overalls, like Boliver. Back inside the room David saw two small red-headed girls run across the floor in nightgowns.

"Honey," Boliver said, turning around and looking

back into the room, "I'm goin' to dig yarbs and make medicine to cure this puppy! Hear me?"

"Boliver, ye ain't had yer breakfast yet," said a woman whom David couldn't see. "Waste a day on a sick hound and not a furrow plowed for corn!"

"Honey, the ground ain't hurtin' none," Boliver said. "I-doggies, I'm on my way!"

Boliver crawled back under the floor of the little log shack where there wasn't any underpinning. David looked under the floor and saw the places on the oak leaves where the hounds had slept. Boliver got his mattock, which could be used for both digging and chopping. On one side of the handle there was a sharp-pointed blade, and on the other there was a hoe.

As they left the house, David watched Boliver walk through the brier patches barefooted. He walked as well as David and his grandmother, who were wearing shoes.

"We've got to find poke root," Boliver told them. "We've got to have bear's-paw, snakeroot, and a lot of other roots, too! And we've got to have some barks! I-doggies, if we don't do something in a hurry, that little hound is a goner!"

"If you can cure my puppy, Mr. Tussie, will you let me bring him to hunt with you?" David asked. "Grandma says you're a great hunter—the best hunter in this valley!"

"David wants to catch a coon, Boliver, so he can have a coonskin cap," Grandma Beverley said.

"I-doggies, this October when the pelts get good, David, we'll ketch a coon," Boliver said. "Only don't you call me 'Mr. Tussie.' That sounds furrin to me. Jist call me Boliver!"

Boliver shook the dirt from the roots of the plant he had found and dug up. He said, "Cynthia, you'll haf to let David carry the puppy so you can carry the roots and bark in yer apron."

"Can we put the roots on Orphan now?" David asked.

"Oh, no, David," Boliver laughed. "We've got to dig a lot of different roots and put 'em in a pot and bile 'em. We'll put the juice on Orphan! Say, why do you call him 'Orphan'?"

"Because I was an orphan until Grandma got me," David replied. "Orphan was an orphan until I got him."

"That makes sense," Boliver said. "That's a purty name fer a hound!"

Then Boliver started digging again. He said: "Bear's-paw."

The plant was waist-high to Boliver and had big, dark-green leaves.

When Boliver walked under the trees and the tree branches swished around his naked shoulders, they didn't leave a mark. He's a tough man, David thought. I'll bet he's a great hunter. David watched Boliver's bare feet smash the greenbrier runners flat on the ground. Briers won't even go into his feet, he thought. Maybe I'll get to be like Boliver. He does look like the pictures of foxes I've seen, but he's a kind man and I love him. He loves hounds and I do, too, and that makes me love Boliver Tussie.

They walked on through the woods, digging roots and

skinning bark from the trees, until Boliver said: "We've got the right roots and barks and we've got enough."

"Boliver, we'll go to my house," Grandma Beverley said. "We'll boil the roots on my stove, and while the roots boil, I'll get your breakfast!"

"I-doggies, that's better," Boliver said. "I see right now I'm goin' to have a young man to hunt with me. When a boy cries over a hound, he's goin' to make a fine man. Cynthia, I've knowed you fer forty years but I didn't know you could love a hound. I've allus knowed you to be a fine woman, but, I-doggies, you're even better than I thought!"

All through the spring, David kept remembering Boliver Tussie's words about Grandma Beverley. And every time he looked at Orphan, he felt a surge of love for his grandmother. She had saved Orphan, and David felt he could never repay her. The first time he got a chance he was going to do something special for her, too. She was the most wonderful woman in the world, and somehow he had to tell her so.

Grandma had certainly been right when she got Boliver Tussie to make medicine to cure the puppy's mange. Soon the hair grew back, and Orphan grew into a pretty tan and white dog.

During the spring months, Orphan grew fast because Grandma Beverley gave him all the milk he could drink. She fed him home-baked bread, and before the summer was over, he was as large as one of Boliver's hounds. Orphan trotted along proudly with his tail in two curls over his back everywhere David went.

When October came, and the leaves changed colors, David, Grandma, and Boliver went to the woods to train Orphan. Grandma had told David that Orphan was a smart puppy and that he would make a good hunting hound. She had been right about this, too. Orphan was soon treeing possums faster than Boliver's hounds. Soon after Orphan treed his first possum, Grandma and David began possum hunting together. On nights when his grandmother was too tired to go, David went into the woods alone with Orphan. The pretty autumn nights with blue skies, moon, and stars did not last long enough for David to do all the hunting he wanted to do. All too quickly, winter came. It was December, and there weren't many good nights for hunting.

LEAF-GATHERING TIME

One morning early in December, as David was carrying in the milk for Grandma Beverley, he suddenly
thought: Before long it'll be Christmas, and at Christmas
I want to make Grandma the happiest woman in the
world! She has been the best person to me that I've ever
known. I want to get her a wonderful present. But how
am I going to get a present without any money? We need
all the money we've got just to live.

David had been thinking about this present since
November. One of the things he had thought about getting for his grandmother was a dress. But he didn't know
how to choose one. His grandmother wore long calico
dresses that she made herself. She didn't dress like the
younger women who lived in the valley. She always wore
dresses with a high collar and with sleeves that came
below her elbows. Her skirts were always full because
his grandmother was a tall woman and took big steps
when she walked.

David's thoughts were interrupted by his grandmother
as he opened the kitchen door.

"David, this is going to be a fair day and we had better gather leaves," Grandma Beverley said, looking from the kitchen window at the rising sun. "We might not have another day in December as fair as today, and we had better get the leaves while they're dry."

"All right, Grandma," David said. He set the big zinc milk bucket on the kitchen table. Then he removed his coonskin cap and watched his grandmother dry the last dish and put it in the cupboard.

"Just as soon as I strain the milk, we'll go, David," Grandma Beverley said.

David stood there with his cap in his hand, watching his grandmother strain the milk into a big crock. Then he carried the milk from the kitchen to the cellar that was dug into the hillside and walled with rocks and covered with a dirt roof. When he returned to get the second crock, Grandma Beverley looked at her tall grandson and said: "When you and I work together, David, we can do just about anything!"

David smiled at his grandmother and picked up the second crock of milk from the table.

"Of course we can, Grandma," he said. "I've never seen anything yet that you and I couldn't do!"

"I'm ready, David," Grandma Beverley said, when David came back from the cellar again. "Let's go to the corn crib and get the rake and a couple of burlap sacks."

Grandma took her long steps, but it wasn't hard now for David to keep up with her. He remembered how he had once had to run to keep up. But now he could walk as fast as she could. When they reached the corn crib, David unfastened the door and went in. He brought out

27

the two sacks and the rake.

"Now, where's the best place to find leaves, David?" Grandma Beverley asked.

"Over there on the hill under the white oak trees," David replied. "There's a little ravine down the face of that hill, and the wind blows the leaves into it. Grandma, the leaves are waist-deep. We won't have to do much raking to get the leaves over there."

"David, you've learned fast," Grandma Beverley said, smiling. "Think of your finding a ravine which the wind has filled with leaves! How did you know it was there?"

"When I was possum hunting the other night, I stepped down into the dry leaves, and sank up to my waist in them," he explained.

They crossed the little stream and started walking up a gentle slope toward the white oaks.

"I don't think we'll need the rake, Grandma," David told her.

"But it won't hurt to bring it along," she said. "We might need it. It might take more leaves than are in the ravine to cover our garden. And, of course, the real dry leaves on top we'll have to put in Daisy's stall. Cows need warm, dry beds."

When they reached the ravine, David ran and jumped into the leaves and sank almost up to his shoulders. He called, "Look how deep they are, Grandma!" Then he quickly started filling his sack with the dry leaves.

"Just a minute, David!" Grandma Beverley said, as she got to the ravine. Let me help you! I'll hold the sack open!"

28

"But you can't get down in this ravine, Grandma," David said.

"Oh, yes, I can," she told him. "And two can fill a sack with leaves better than one!"

When Grandma Beverley waded down into the deep bed of leaves, David smiled. She held the sack against her side with her elbow and stretched it out with her hand. Then with her other hand she pulled the other side of the sack until she made a triangular opening. This made the opening large enough for David to gather a great armload of leaves and put them in.

"Grandma, I never saw anybody hold a sack open like that before," David said.

"Your Grandpa Beverley and I used to gather leaves together," she said. "He showed me how to hold a sack open this way. How do you hold a sack open, David?"

"Well, Grandma, I put one corner of it between my teeth and then I use both hands," he explained, as he put a second armload of leaves through the big opening. "I watched Boliver Tussie hold a sack open the first night we caught a possum. That's how Boliver held the sack open for me to put the possum in."

Then Grandma Beverley laughed, almost as loudly as the sound of the wind in the dry leaves still clinging to the boughs of the tough-butted white oaks.

"You've taught me something, Grandma," he said. "I didn't like to put the sack between my teeth to hold it. I wondered if the sack was dirty. But I put it there just the same. I'll never do that again."

"You've taught me something, too, David," she said.

"I never thought about letting the wind rake leaves for me. Your Grandpa Beverley did all his work the easy way, but he never thought of your way. We used to go to the woods and rake the leaves with our garden rake. We'd rake up big heaps, and then we'd carry them to the garden and spread them, and we'd take some of them to the stable and bed the stalls. But it is a lot easier and faster to have the leaves already raked!"

David was pleased that he had found something his Grandma Beverley didn't know. He pushed the leaves down lightly in the sack so he could put another armload in. "These leaves are dry as gunpowder, Grandma," he said. "They'll make good bedding for Daisy's stall."

"Yes," Grandma Beverley said. "Daisy will love to sleep on these dry leaves. Down under the dry leaves, we'll find wet ones. Wet leaves will be better than the dry ones to spread over the garden. If we get a wind tonight, the wet leaves won't blow away."

David and Grandma Beverley filled their sacks and then started walking back down the gentle slope toward the little stream. The sun was high in the blue sky, and the wind was soft and warm for December. The long coon's tail on David's cap rode on the wind above the sack across his shoulder.

"This is the right time to gather leaves, David," Grandma Beverley said. "Tomorrow we might have rain or snow. This is the time of year for foul weather. Just think, it's only eighteen more days until Christmas! I want this to be a good Christmas for you. You've been a fine boy, David. I don't know what I'd have ever done

31

if I had been left alone without you."

"I hope it's going to be a good Christmas for you, too, Grandma," David said. "You've been good to me."

They walked silently up to the stable, and David poured his sack of leaves over the partition into Daisy's stall. Then Grandma Beverley gave David her sack of leaves, and he poured them over, too. All the time they were working, David was thinking about what his grandmother had just said about Christmas.

I know what I can do to make money to get Grandma a present, David thought, as they walked back to get another load of leaves. He was swinging his empty burlap sack in the wind. Why haven't I thought of it before? The first pretty, warm night when there's not a wind blowing to scare the possums, I can take Orphan to the woods and catch a sackful. I can cure the pelts in a hurry and sell them to the Darby Produce House. That's the way I'll get a Christmas present for Grandma! I hope a soft, warm night comes in a hurry. If it does, I'll get Grandma's present, all right!

Fifteen Days Until Christmas

This will be the night, David thought, as he pushed back from the supper table. This is the night for possums and coons to stir. It's the warm, soft night I've been waiting for! Orphan and I will catch the possums tonight!

"Grandma, I must be going," David said as he got up from the table. "This will be a good night to hunt."

"But we have plenty of meat in the smokehouse, David," his Grandma Beverley said. "We've got plenty of pork. We don't need any wild meat!"

"But, Grandma, it's such a fine night to hunt," David said. "When it's a warm, still night and the ground is damp, the possums stir. When the wind is blowing, it shakes the dead leaves on the white oaks and rustles the leaves on the ground, and that scares the possums. Tonight, the possums will go to the pawpaw bushes and the persimmon trees. And Orphan has been wanting to go for several nights!"

"Good luck to you, David," she said, smiling as he picked up his lantern. "I hope you catch a possum!"

"Won't you go along with me, Grandma?" he asked her.

"No, I'd better not go tonight," she said. "I'm afraid I can't climb over the hills as fast as I used to. I might not be able to keep up with you and Orphan! You'll get along better without me tonight."

David looked at his grandmother and smiled. If you only knew why I am going, Grandma, he thought. But you don't.

When Orphan saw David with a lighted lantern, he knew what was up. He came running toward him, and he jumped up and rested his front paws on his sweater. He looked up into David's face and whined. Orphan was pleased that David was taking him hunting.

"You know when it's a good night to hunt, don't you, Orphan?" David said kindly to his hound.

He looked down at Orphan's shiny coat of short white and tan hair. "Orphan, you're the prettiest hound in the valley now," David said, as he patted his head. "And you're the best hound in the valley, too!"

Orphan barked at David. He was ready to go hunting.

"We'll be on our way in just a minute, Orphan," David told him.

Then David walked to the corn crib where he opened the door and got a coffee sack and a mattock.

"If a possum goes in a hole, Orphan"—David talked to his hound—"I'll dig him out. I don't want you digging and pulling at the rocks and roots with your teeth. You'll break 'em off. I want you to keep your teeth as long as you live. You won't be able to fight wild game without them. When a dog loses his teeth, he is in bad shape. If a possum goes up a tree, I'll climb it and get him. You know how I can climb, Orphan."

The hound whined, and barked as if he had understood what David was telling him.

When they had walked away from the house, David spoke to his dog again. "Orphan, I want you to find at least three possums tonight. I want to skin them for their pelts. I want to sell the pelts to the Darby Produce House in Blakesburg and get some money, for I want to buy Grandma Beverley a Christmas present. Do you understand, Orphan? See, we can't talk about this in front of Grandma!"

Orphan whined and barked again as he looked up into David's face.

"Now, go find a possum," David said. "It's only fifteen days until Christmas and we'll have to hurry!"

Orphan ran away stiff-legged into the warm darkness. His nose was in the air and he was sniffing something as he ran.

He's winding something, David thought, as he hurried along in the direction Orphan was running. But the dog was soon out of sight up the valley.

When David heard Orphan bark a few minutes later, he stopped in his tracks. His heart beat faster while Orphan's barks grew louder and faster.

It's a possum all right, he thought, as he waited and listened. He's getting closer to it.

Suddenly, Orphan stopped barking, but only for a few seconds before he started again. He had changed the sound of his barking.

"He's treed it!" David shouted, as he took off running in the direction of the sound.

David ran under the tall poplars, where the golden leaves were almost knee-deep, but they were damp and didn't rustle under his feet. He leaped across a little stream, and ran alongside a fence until he came to the place where Orphan was barking. The hound was standing on his hind legs with his front paws on the trunk of a little sourwood. David crawled between the wires of the fence to get to the tree. Then he held his lantern above his head.

"I see him, Orphan!" he said. "You can see him, too! There's a big possum up there holding to a little grapevine! I'll shake him down! Now, don't you bite him unless he tries to run!"

Orphan barked faster than he breathed. When David took hold of the grapevine, the dog knew what he was going to do. David gave it a little shake, but the possum held on. As he shook the grapevine harder, Orphan stopped barking. David looked up into the tree and his eyes shone brighter than stars as he watched the possum tumbling down like a big, gray ball. Just as soon as he fell to the ground, David grabbed him by his long tail and held him up so Orphan couldn't bite him. The possum was limp, and seemed to be dead.

"You're just 'playing possum'," David said, as he felt his weight. "It never hurt you to fall from that little tree. Besides, I didn't let Orphan bite you!"

Orphan leaped up, trying to bite the possum.

"Behave, Orphan!" David told him. "I don't want your teeth to make a hole through his skin. I want this one

36

to make a good pelt. I want it to bring over a dollar. He's a nice possum, with a pretty coat of fur!"

"Here's one to buy you a Christmas present, Grandma," David said, smiling as he put the possum into the sack. "Now go on, Orphan, and tree another one. We have to catch three possums tonight. I'll have to skin 'em and cure the pelts before I can sell 'em to Darby's Produce House. We have to hurry. Go tree another possum!"

Orphan ran up the valley, while David lifted the coffee sack up and down, feeling the weight of the possum. It was no longer pretending to be dead, but was climbing up the sack. While David was shaking the possum down to the bottom of the sack, he heard his dog bark again. David could barely hear him. He started running in the direction of the sound.

When David found Orphan, he was at the bottom of a cliff, barking under the rock.

"It's a possum, all right," David said. "But, Orphan, we can't get him! He's a smart possum, and he knows where to hide!"

Orphan didn't want to leave the cliff.

"Come on, Orphan," David said. "Come on! I'm leaving! Let's go to the pawpaws and the persimmon trees! There aren't any rock cliffs over there!"

Orphan whined when he came away to follow David.

"You're crying, Orphan," David said. "No use to cry over a possum we can't get!"

Orphan seemed to understand. He stopped whining and ran off into the darkness. As he ran away, he was sniffing the warm night wind.

He smells something, David thought, as he sat down to rest on a rock. I'll wait and see what he does.

He didn't have long to wait before Orphan barked again, this time from the other side of the north wall of the valley, beyond Wince Leffard Gap.

He's close to that possum, too, David thought, as he started running toward the distant sound.

Orphan's barks were sweet music to his ears. When he reached Wince Leffard Gap, he was getting his breath hard and fast. He stopped and listened to the hound's long, soft barks above the pounding of his heart. Orphan was barking up a tree in the cliffs above Academy Branch. David started running again, toward the sound. He leaped over the small rocks and climbed over the cliffs. He went through wild grapevine thickets. And he came to places in the woods where the last year's winter sleet had broken the tops from the trees. Here were great piles of dead treetops that he had to work his way through. But he finally reached Orphan. The hound was standing with his paws up on the short stub of a poplar tree, which had fallen in a wind storm. He was barking without stopping for breath.

"Oh, look what a possum, Orphan!" David cried with joy, as he looked up. The possum was sitting on top of the short tree stub, just barely above Orphan's reach. "Take it easy, Orphan! I'll climb up there and get him by the tail!"

David hung his lantern on a little broken limb so he would have light. Then he climbed the tree a few feet, reached up and got hold of the possum's tail. He slid down, holding the possum by the tail.

"Look what a possum, Orphan!" he said, as Orphan leaped up. "No, you can't have him! This is another fine pelt for Grandma's present!"

When David untied the sack and put this possum in, the two possums started fighting. He shook the sack to make them behave. Then he put it across his shoulder, picked up his mattock and lantern, and called Orphan.

"Let's get one more, Orphan," he said, looking for his dog. But Orphan was gone.

He left here in a hurry, David thought. Then he looked

at the bark on a tree near him. It was a persimmon tree.

He's after another possum, David thought. They've come here to eat persimmons.

When he heard Orphan bark, the sound was so faint he thought the hound was beyond another hill. He started again in the direction of the sound through tangled treetops, briers, and wild grapevines. When he went over a steep bank and down into a deep ravine, he found Orphan barking under another cliff. This cliff was not more than a hundred yards from where Orphan had treed the last possum, but the dog had sounded far away.

"Come on, Orphan!" David said. "We can't get that one!"

Orphan didn't want to come, but when David started climbing up the steep hill toward Laurel Ridge, he left the cliff.

When David looked up the steep hill, he could see the stars shining through the dense timber. They looked as if they were about ten feet above Laurel Ridge. He kept on climbing toward them but the higher he got, the farther away they were.

"Now, Orphan," he said, when they reached Laurel Ridge, "we're in tall timber. We ought to get another possum here!"

They walked more than a mile around Laurel Ridge. Orphan would hunt first one side of the ridge and then the other. He didn't strike a trail until they reached Sulphur Spring, which was below Laurel Ridge. Then he barked his trailing bark in the deep, dark woods. David waited, and didn't start toward him until he heard him change his bark. Orphan barked faster when he treed a possum.

When David got down the steep hill to Orphan, he found him barking excitedly up a giant oak.

Can I climb this one? he wondered. He wasn't sure.

But he tied his possums up in a tree so Orphan couldn't bite them through the sack, and he put his belt through the lantern bales and let it rest on his back. Then he started climbing the giant oak. He couldn't reach all around the tree, but he held onto its rough bark until he climbed to the first limb. He rested, and then he climbed on until he saw a big object near the top that looked like a squirrel's nest made of leaves.

This is a big tree for a possum to climb, he thought.

When David got higher into the top of the big oak, he stopped and took his lantern from his belt. He held it above his head to look at the big object that was moving restlessly up there.

It's not a possum, he thought. It's too big, and its coat is darker. Then he saw that it had a big, bushy tail with dark rings around it. "It's a coon!" he shouted.

David watched the big raccoon open his mouth and bare his teeth. Then the coon walked out on a long limb in the top of the giant tree.

That limb might split off with me if I try to follow him, David thought. I'm nearly up to the stars here. But that coon's hide would buy a nice Christmas present for Grandma.

David looked at the coon out on the limb. This was the first coon Orphan had ever treed. "I hate to leave

41

you, but I'll have to," he said.

Then David put his lantern on his belt again and started back down the tree. When he reached the ground his hands were hot and his legs smarted where he had rubbed them against the rough oak bark.

"He's up there all right, Orphan," David said. "He's as big as you are, but we can't get him. He's too far out on that limb. I was afraid it would break with me and I'd fall to the ground. Grandma would never know where to find me unless you'd tell her. You can't talk to Grandma like I can."

He patted Orphan's head as the dog looked up into the tree and barked.

"We'll have to leave him, Orphan," David said. "We'll have to come back sometime and you can put him up a smaller tree."

Just as they had walked down Sulphur Spring Hollow and reached the valley, Orphan ran ahead of David as fast as he could go. He ran across the pasture field and barked up a little redbud tree. David walked over to where a little possum was hanging just out of Orphan's reach. He reached up and got the possum, which was not even as large as a squirrel. "You're the third possum, all right," he said. "You're a baby possum."

David opened the sack and put the little possum in with the big ones. Then he started for home. Orphan trotted ahead of him, with his long red tongue hanging from his mouth.

A Hunter Ruled By His Heart

Killing a possum just for its hide, David thought, as he walked along behind Orphan . . . killing a baby possum. We don't need wild meat. We've got plenty of meat in the smokehouse. Grandma won't eat possum, anyway.

Then he walked on slowly, thinking how the possums lived in hollow logs, cliffs, and dirt holes. He thought about how they had to hunt food at night from persimmon trees, pawpaw bushes, and old apple orchards. They must often go hungry, he thought, as he stopped and took the sack from his shoulder. He untied the sack and looked at the three possums. "If I kill you," he said to the possums, "I'll only get your hides. Kill you for your hides! Every time I wear this coonskin cap, I think of the night Boliver shot the coon from the tree! I think of how much more the skin was worth to the coon than it is to me."

David sat there looking at the possums.

"Little one, I'm going to turn you loose," he said, looking at the tiny possum. "I know I'm not going to kill you for your little hide. It wouldn't be worth twenty-five cents. I'm going to let you go back to your mother. And I don't want to kill you either," he said softly to the big possums that were looking up at him with fear in their bright, beady eyes. "Grandma wouldn't want me to kill you for your hides. I'll find another way to buy her a present."

Then David closed the sack and put it over his shoulder.

"Shucks, what's the matter with me?" David grumbled to himself. "I've helped Boliver kill possums and never thought anything about it. Now I catch possums to buy Grandma a present and start thinking about how much they need their hides!"

I've got a bee tree to cut yet, he thought. I can sell enough honey to buy Grandma a present. I'm going to turn these possums loose when I find the right place.

When David came to a tree with a bushy top, he stopped. He opened the sack and lifted out a big possum by the tail and set him on the side of the tree. Then he let the possum scamper up to his freedom. He caught the second possum by the tail and put it in the tree, too. Then he reached down into the sack and caught the little possum around the neck with his hand. He put it up high into the tree where it climbed slowly up and sat down on the first limb, while the two big ones climbed into the top twigs that swayed to and fro with them in the starlight.

"I feel better," he said to himself. "Come on, Orphan, let's go home."

"David, did you and Orphan get a possum last night?" Grandma Beverley asked.

"We got three possums—and Orphan treed the biggest coon I've ever seen!"

"Where, David?"

"In the biggest oak in Sulphur Spring Hollow," he told her. "It went out on a limb and I couldn't follow. I was afraid the limb would break."

"What if you had fallen from that tree?" she asked. "I worried about you last night. I kept thinking: 'What if something happens to David? What will I do? How can I do without him?' David, I could hardly go to sleep for thinking about you out there hunting possums."

"I know, Grandma . . ." he began, but didn't finish.

"Yes, you like to get out and hunt with Orphan," she interrupted. "I know you like to hunt alone. I know you're not afraid in the woods at night. And I want you to stay that way. But I don't want you to get so venturesome that you will walk out on a limb in the top of an oak after a coon. What if you had, and the limb had split off with you and you had fallen? I couldn't have found you."

"I thought about that last night, Grandma," David said. "I wanted the coon, but I didn't take a chance. I'm careful about risking my life, Grandma."

"What did you do with your possums, David?"

David turned to his grandmother and said, "I turned 'em loose."

"Why, David?"

"Grandma, I'm getting so I hate to kill a possum,"

46

he said. "The only way to kill one is to break its neck. I have to put a stick over its neck and put a foot on each end of the stick and pull on its tail."

"I've always been bothered by that, too, David," she said. "Your Grandfather Beverley got so he wouldn't kill a possum. He said he always hated to hear one struggle for breath after its neck was broken."

"Orphan treed a baby possum last night," David said. "And I got to thinking about killing it for its hide. I thought it needed its skin more than I needed twenty-five cents. When I looked down at it in the sack, I started thinking about the others, too. This is their valley, too, I thought. They live here and love this valley and they have a hard time finding something to eat. They must get awful hungry at times, I thought. I started thinking a lot about this. It was the first time in my life I felt that way. So I turned them all loose."

"David, you did right," Grandma said. "I'm proud of you. You're going to make as fine a man as your Grandfather Beverley. And he was the best man I ever knew."

47

Ten Days Until Christmas

"Now get into the corn crib, Orphan," David said. "I'm not going possum hunting tonight. I'm going to chop down a tree. It might fall on you." Orphan went inside the crib, and David closed the door. Then he hurried to the house.

"Grandma," he asked, "have you any old rags you're not going to use?"

"Yes, David. What do you want with them?"

"I need them for my bee smoker."

"Are you going to cut your bee tree in December?"

"Yes, Grandma."

"But I thought you were planning to wait until next spring so you could save the bees!"

"We have twelve beehives around the garden," he said. "And we don't have any honey."

"That's right," she admitted. "We needed money and we had to sell our honey."

Cynthia Beverley turned from the dishes she was putting in the cupboard. She said: "There are some rags upstairs I've saved for rugs. I'll get them for you."

While she went upstairs to get the rags, David got his

lantern from the nail on the wall behind the cookstove. He took the globe off and wiped it clean with a damp cloth. The night he had gone possum hunting, he had tilted the lantern when he jumped over some rocks and had smoked the globe.

I'll have to have a clean lantern globe to see how to rob the bees, he thought. I'll have to have a nice even flame to give light when I cut the tree.

Then he took a pair of scissors and trimmed the charred end of the lantern wick. He put more oil into his lantern from the gallon coaloil can his grandmother kept near the stovewood box in the kitchen. He had the lantern ready when his grandmother came down the stairs with a handful of wool rags.

"David, we had to sell all of our honey last summer," she said. "I know how well you and I like honey for breakfast, too. The money paid our taxes."

"Grandma, I can do without honey," David said. "I didn't mind when you sold it. I know we had to pay our taxes."

"Is Boliver Tussie going to help you cut the tree?"

"No, I'm going to cut it myself."

"It's a big tree, isn't it?"

"Yes, but I can chop it down."

"I'm going with you, David. We'll saw the tree down together."

"Grandma, I can cut the tree and rob the bees. You don't have to go."

"Years ago, I used to help your Grandpa Beverley cut bee trees," she said. "We always had a bee tree to cut late in the fall or early in the winter. I'd go with him and we'd saw the tree down. Then he'd rob the bees and we'd get a few stings. Your grandpa would laugh and I'd laugh, too. We'd get a big water bucket full of pretty golden honey. I'm going with you tonight, David. I wouldn't miss this for anything. Seems like honey from autumn flowers is always better."

GRANDMA WALKS IN THE WIND

David left the house with a crosscut saw, ax, and bee smoker. His Grandma Beverley carried the lantern, two large buckets, and a handful of rags. She had a knife in one of the buckets to cut the honey from the hollow tree.

"These are the bees I found watering on a sandbar down in the pasture," David said, as they walked along the path, enjoying the clear, cool December night. "I coursed them right up the hill yonder to a big hollow white oak. That was the easiest bee tree I've ever found. There are a lot of bees in the tree, too. They fly in and out of a knothole high on the tree like a small, bright cloud. You might get a lot of stings by coming along, Grandma."

"Bees will hardly ever sting me," she answered. "What if they do? I've been stung a few times before, and I don't mind a few more stings."

"What, Grandma?" David asked her. "You mean you're not afraid of bee stings?"

"I said I didn't mind getting a few stings," she said. "David, one time the joint was swollen on my finger until

I couldn't get my wedding ring off. Then a wasp stung me on the hand, and my, how it hurt! But it made the swelling go down, and I could slip my ring over my finger. Now I've got rheumatism again and my finger joints are swollen. So I want a few bee stings to make the swelling go down."

"Shucks, Grandma," David said. "I didn't know bee stings were good for anything. You know so many things!"

"It's the truth, Son," she said. "Bee stings are good for swelling in the joints."

Grandma Beverley took long steps, swinging her lighted lantern. Millions of bright stars twinkled in the clear blue sky to give the dark earth some light. Soon they walked into the leafless timber.

"It's this way, Grandma," David said. "Follow me."

The trees were so tall that, looking up from the ground, David could believe that their top-most twigs were right against the stars. He and his grandmother walked over the carpet of last year's leaves that rustled beneath their feet. There were a few brown leaves clinging to the boughs of the white oaks and the light wind rustled them and made a lonesome sound.

"We've reached the white oak grove, Grandma," David said. "The tree is right down here."

David walked down to the big white oak that leaned down the hill. He laid his hand upon its bark. "This is the tree, Grandma," he said. "See my initial on it!"

His grandmother walked up to the tree and looked at the big "D" that David had cut in the white oak's bark with his ax.

"Yes, mark a bee tree and no one else is allowed to cut it," she said. "And this tree is in our woods, David."

Blossoms For The Bees

David broke a branch from a little dogwood and hung his lantern handle over the stub so its light would shine on the white oak.

"Now, Grandma, this will be harder than sawing wood," David told her. "Reckon you can hold out to cut this tree?"

"Oh, yes, David," she said, smiling. "I'll take my time. We'll saw it faster than you could chop it down."

David and his grandmother held the saw against the bark of the white oak. Then they began pulling it across the tree. Slivers of green wood soon came from the drag teeth as the saw ate deeper into the tree. Once Grandma Beverley stopped to rest. She stood up straight to rest her back, because, when she pulled the crosscut saw, she had to bend over. After she had rested, they began sawing again.

"Grandma, you can saw as good as anybody I've ever sawed with," David said. "I believe you can saw better than Boliver."

"Thank you, David," she said. "I used to help your grandpa. We used to saw down trees and cut them up for wood. It was a lot of fun, too!"

Soon the tree started cracking and there was a big split in its trunk. David and his grandmother pulled the saw out and stepped back out of the way.

"It's going, Grandma!" David shouted, as the big tree started slipping down through the other trees to the ground. There was a great swish and the popping of branches, and then the white oak hit the ground with a loud crash.

"The bees will be all excited," Grandma Beverley said. "They won't know what's happened to their tree. The jolt will wake them from their sleep. I'll fill the bee smoker with rags while they get settled."

In the stillness of the night they could hear the disturbed bees making a humming noise down inside the hollow tree. Grandma Beverley filled the bee smoker with rags, struck a match, and held it to them. Then she worked the smoker until the foul-smelling smoke started puffing out. "It's ready, David," she said. "We're ready to get some fresh wild honey!"

"Grandma, I believe there's plenty of honey in this tree," David said. "It's big enough to hold a lot."

"I remember once when your Grandpa Beverley and I got a whole tub of honey from a tree," she said. "That was a long time ago when there were plenty of wild flowers, when the bees had plenty of blossoms to work on. Our hills hadn't been plowed up then, and people were more careful with fire. No one ever let out a fire to kill the wild flowers and trees that bloomed for the bees."

"You use the smoker, Grandma," David said, "and I'll chop a hole into the tree to get the honey."

"We won't waste the honey, David, if I help you saw places into the tree and then you split them out with your ax," she said. "That's the way your Grandpa Beverley and I used to do."

"But I'm afraid you'll get tired," David said.

"Oh, no, David," his grandmother said. "That was an easy tree to saw down. I'm not tired."

Robbing The Bees

Grandma Beverley took the lantern from the dogwood sapling and held the bee smoker while David carried the saw and ax. They walked beside the trunk of the tree until they were about fifty feet down the hill. "Here are the bees, David!" Grandma Beverley said. They were flying from a big knothole and swarming around the lantern light. "Look at them! They're the big golden honey bees that make a lot of honey!"

Then Grandma Beverley set the lantern on the ground beside her. She put the bee smoker up to the knothole and began pumping smoke back into the log. "This will slow 'em down," she said.

Grandma Beverley smoked the bees until they were too sick to fly out of the knothole. David plugged the opening with sticks and leaves so they couldn't crawl out. Then he hung the lantern in a small sourwood so it could furnish enough light for Grandma and him to saw into the log.

They sawed down into the log in three places. They sawed deep enough to reach the honey, for they saw it sticking on the teeth of the saw.

"Now, before you split these pieces out of the tree, David," she said, "you unstop the knothole and I'll give them some more smoke! If I don't, when you split out a chunk of the tree, they'll cover us!"

David pulled the sticks and leaves from the knothole and his grandmother pumped more ragsmoke back into the hollow tree until the great roar of the disturbed bees became quieter. Then David began splitting the first chunk from the oak.

"David, you can use an ax like a man," his grandmother said proudly, as she watched him lift the chunk from the tree.

"We've got some honey, Grandma!" he shouted excitedly. "Here's plenty of it!"

"We need more smoke, too," she said, as the bees started coming out. She got up close and smoked the bees.

"Ouch! One stung me on the hand!" she said, laughing. "But that's good! I hope one stings my other hand!"

"One got up my pants leg and stung me, too!" David said, slapping his leg where the bee had stung him. David turned the chunk over and it was covered with honeycomb three tiers deep. "Give me the buckets, Grandma," he said.

Grandma Beverley stopped using her smoker long enough to give David the buckets. David stripped the honey from the chunk first. Then he started taking honey from the tree while his grandmother began smoking the bees again. When a bee stung David, he laughed and told his grandmother, and when one stung her, she laughed and told him.

He took enough honey from this section to fill a bucket.

"That's the prettiest honey I ever saw," Grandma Beverley said. "David, you'll like this honey for your breakfast. Honey made in the fall is mostly made from yellow blossoms. It's strange, but wild flowers in late summer and early fall nearly all have yellow blossoms, and they make pretty golden honey."

David split the second section from the log. Then he filled the second big bucket.

"There's plenty more honey, Grandma," he said. "We didn't bring enough buckets! What will we do now?"

"But we've got six gallons of honey, David!" she said.

"This will be enough. We can leave the rest for the bees. You can put the chunks back onto the tree."

"Yes, I can, Grandma," he said. "I'd never have thought of doing that!"

"That's the reason I thought it would be better to use the saw."

"Now we won't lose the bees, will we?" David asked.

"No, we'll save the bees," she said.

David put back the two pieces he had split from the tree, and they fitted together neatly.

"Now, tomorrow we can come back and seal the cracks where we've sawed so the rain can't get into them," Grandma Beverley said. "I've got plenty of sealing wax. The bees can live here all winter, and come spring, we can put them in a hive!"

"Gee, Grandma, this is wonderful!" David said. "I hated to cut this tree because of losing the bees. You do know how to cut a bee tree, don't you?"

"Oh, yes," she said. "I remember how your Grandpa Beverley and I used to cut them a long time ago. We used to save bees in the fall by cutting the tree this way. Of course, if the tree split all to pieces when it fell, we couldn't save the bees."

"But, Grandma," David said, rubbing a spot on his hand where a bee had stung him, "how will we get home with this load?"

"We'll take the honey, the lantern, and the smoker, and come back for the tools tomorrow," she said. "We have to come back and seal the cracks in the tree tomorrow, anyway."

Honey That's Not For Money

David picked up the two big buckets of honey, and his grandmother got the lantern and the bee smoker. David walked up the hill slowly, swaying under the weight of the buckets. His grandmother walked behind him with the lantern to light the way.

"Be careful not to catch your toe on something and stumble, David," she warned. "Don't fall and spill the honey! Be sure-footed, David."

"I'll be sure-footed, Grandma," he grunted. "I've trained myself to be careful when I climb over the rock cliffs at night when I'm possum hunting."

"That honey will come in handy!" she said. "That's honey we're not going to sell."

"But Grandma . . . ," David started to say.

"I know, David," she interrupted him, "this is a lot of honey, but we'll need it. You need honey for your breakfast, and I need it in the winter for colds! I'm awful glad you found this tree and kept it until now. It's God's blessing that you did, David. I'll need honey this winter for my coughing. And we'll use it for baking when we don't have sugar."

David walked silently with the buckets until they reached the cleared pasture field. Then he set the buckets down and rested himself.

"How many stings did you get, Grandma?" he asked her.

"Seven," she said. "How many did you get?"

"Five," he said, as he picked up the buckets again.

"It takes us to rob the bees, doesn't it, David?" she said. "Just think how you have learned to find wild bees, and just think of the things you can do with your hands! And you have so much fun doing them! David, I don't know what I would do without you."

SEVEN MORE DAYS

As David walked over the snow three days later, carrying two buckets of milk for Mrs. Orville Byrd, he thought about the present he wanted to get for his grandmother. He milked two cows every night and morning for Mrs. Byrd and he made fifty cents a day for doing this. David gave this money to Grandma Beverley. Prices had gone up on everything, and with his hound dog, Orphan, to feed, it took more money for him and his grandmother to live. As he walked, the December snow crunched beneath his feet, and the winter wind sang lonesome, wordless songs in the leafless apple tree boughs over his head. I can't get a dress for Grandma, he thought. She doesn't need a water bucket — we have two. I can't get dishes, either.

David didn't know where to get pretty dishes like those he had seen in Mrs. Byrd's dining room. He had been in her dining room twice. Once she invited him in out of a storm. Once she called him in and told him what to do with the milk when she and Mr. Byrd were going away for the weekend.

When David took the milk to the cellar on this cold

winter evening, Mrs. Byrd opened the kitchen door and said: "Come in, David, after you've finished with the milk. I want to see you before you leave."

David put the milk in the separator. He almost raised a sweat in the warm cellar as he turned the separator by hand. Then he poured the cream in one can, and the skimmed milk in another, as he had always done. He washed the separator and then he went into the house to see what Mrs. Byrd wanted.

"David," she said, "I was talking to Mr. Byrd last night and he wants you to cut a cord of stovewood for us. You've been a good worker for us, the best we've ever had to milk our cows and take care of the milk."

"When do you want me to chop the stovewood, Mrs. Byrd?" he asked, his face beaming. Here is my chance to make some money, he thought quickly.

"Not until after the Christmas holidays," she said.

"Oh, all right, Mrs. Byrd," he said slowly. David was so disappointed he could hardly speak.

Mrs. Byrd was sitting before her kitchen fireplace. She had a piece of cloth on her lap. It was cloth that looked familiar to David. As she talked to him, she had never stopped raveling threads. She was working on a big cloth, going round and round the square, raveling threads and tying fringes. On a little round table near her, there was a small pile of little square pieces of the old wine-bottles design, which was also in the big square she was working on.

"Mrs. Byrd, I don't want to ask you a silly question," David said, "but I've seen that cloth someplace!"

65

"You certainly have," she said, laughing. "You saw it down at the barn! It's a feed sack."

"What are you making?" he asked.

"A tablecloth and napkins," she replied. "With just two feed sacks of the same color, I'll be able to make a tablecloth and nine napkins."

"Oh, they're beautiful!" David said, so quickly that Mrs. Byrd stopped her work and looked up at him. "I'd like to know how to make them!"

"Pull up a chair and I'll show you," she said.

Mrs. Byrd was pleased that David was interested.

"See, David, the sack is sewed up," she said, picking up a sack at her feet. "First, you shake the loose feed out of it."

"Shouldn't you wash it first?" David asked.

"If you do, it won't fringe as easily," she told him.

"Turn it wrong side out," she said, turning the sack. "Start unraveling it at this corner."

She unraveled the sack to show him how.

"That's simple!" David said. "I can do that!"

"Sure you can," she smiled.

David watched Mrs. Byrd closely.

"The sack has two selvage sides, see," she said. "Tear them off so the sack will ravel."

The selvage edges of the sack were woven to prevent raveling.

Then Mrs. Byrd showed David how to unravel the sacks and tie the fringes. She showed him how to take one sack, divide it into three equal parts, then take each one of these pieces and divide it into three equal parts.

66

These pieces would be the napkins.

"Will you sell me two of the empty sacks down at the barn?" David asked. There was a new light in his eyes.

"Go hunt yourself two of the prettiest sacks down

there," she answered. "I'll give them to you."

"Thank you, Mrs. Byrd," David said, leaving her kitchen in a hurry.

David knew that he and his grandmother didn't have any sacks at their house. He had never seen feed-sack tablecloths and napkins before. But he knew that if Mrs. Byrd made them, they were all right. She had the prettiest house in the valley. People came to visit just to see her home.

David went to the big wooden box in the barn where the empty feed sacks had been thrown. Soon he found two of the prettiest sacks he'd ever seen. They were printed in the autumn oak-leaf design. He knew these were the right choices, for his Grandma Beverley had always loved the October days when the leaves turned and the lazy autumn winds swirled them down.

That night, after Grandma Beverley had gone to bed, David sat up and worked on his tablecloth and napkins. This was a new kind of work for him. He was very slow at first and he found the tying of the threads very difficult. But he kept on working, and the longer he worked, the easier his work became. He got the tablecloth finished in three nights. On the fourth and fifth nights he sat up after his grandmother had gone to bed and made six of his napkins. He worked each night until midnight. Grandma Beverley was fast asleep and never knew when David went to bed. On the sixth night, he finished the last three napkins. "Talk about something pretty!" he said to himself. Then he took them into the kitchen and placed them over the oilcloth on the table.

Grandma will surely love these, he thought.

The next morning, when David went to milk for Mrs. Byrd, he took along his tablecloth and napkins. After he'd milked the cows and separated the milk, he showed them to Mrs. Byrd.

"David, this is the prettiest tablecloth and napkins I've ever seen," she said. "You have good taste. You selected sacks I have overlooked. How perfectly beautiful!"

When David told her what he was going to do with them, and how he had made them while his grandmother slept, tears came to Mrs. Byrd's eyes. "You won't have to wash and iron them after she goes to bed," Mrs. Byrd told him. "I'll wash and iron them for you. I'll put them in a nice box and wrap them, too."

That evening, after David finished milking, he went to the house and knocked on Mrs. Byrd's door. She opened it and gave him the box, wrapped in Christmas paper. "I have a little present for you, too, David," she said. "I have a little pig out there in a box on the back porch. It's a runt pig. Our sow had fifteen, one more than she could feed."

"Oh, thank you, Mrs. Byrd!" David said. "Your fixing Grandma's present was enough for me, but you couldn't have given me a nicer Christmas present than a pig! Now Grandma won't have to buy us a pig next year!"

David took the present for Grandma Beverley and the box with the pig. When he got home, he put the pig in the corn crib. Then he slipped up to his room while his grandmother was in the kitchen. David was as happy as he had ever been in his life.

It was one of the coldest Christmas Eves they'd ever had in the valley. The snow was a foot deep, and the wind had drifted small white ridges of snow against the fences.

"We are too poor to have much of a Christmas, David," Grandma Beverley said with a smile. "This will be a cold Christmas night, too."

"I have a present Mrs. Byrd gave me to show you in the morning," David said. "I'll mend the fire so we'll have fire all night. This is the coldest Christmas I can remember, Grandma."

When his grandmother went to bed, David pretended he was going to bed, too. He went upstairs to his room and waited until he was sure she was asleep. Then he slipped into her room and found her shoes under the side of her bed. He put the box on top of her shoes.

CHRISTMAS IN THE VALLEY

The next morning David was up early and rekindled the fire from the live embers. The bluster of mad winds roared around their house and banged their gates. It moaned through the branches of the leafless sassafras that stood beside the well in their back yard. It was Christmas at their house, all right. One of David's socks was filled with two bananas, an orange, and striped candy, and the other sock was filled with mixed nuts. These were the things David had looked forward to getting since he had known there was a Christmas.

After he made a fire in the kitchen stove, David went out to feed the chickens and cow. This was Christmas morning and he was feeding early. He wanted to give his grandmother time to get up and get dressed.

When David came in from feeding, his face felt numb from the raw winter wind. He carried a box into the house. Grandma Beverley was up and dressed and sitting before the fire. She had the tablecloth and napkins on her lap.

"David, look," Grandma Beverley said softly, tears coming from her eyes and rolling down her wrinkled

71

face. "I wonder where this nice tablecloth and napkins came from?"

"I made them myself from feed sacks," David said proudly. "Mrs. Byrd showed me how."

"They're the prettiest things I ever saw in my life," Grandma Beverley said. "Who in the world would have ever thought of making a tablecloth and napkins out of feed sacks!"

Grandma Beverley fondled the tablecloth and napkins the way a little girl fondles her dolls on Christmas morning.

"David, what have you got in that box?" his grandmother asked. "It couldn't be a pig I hear grunting?"

"That's what it is, Grandma!" he said happily. "It's a Christmas present from Mr. and Mrs. Byrd. Their sow had fifteen pigs, one more than the sow could feed. So she gave me the runt pig for Christmas!"

"Oh, that's wonderful, David," she said, looking down in the box at the little white pig. "Runt pigs make the finest hogs. We'll feed him after you look at your presents. Go back there and look on the dresser."

When David went into his grandmother's room with her and looked on her dresser, he shouted, "Oh, Grandma!" and set his box with the pig in it on the floor. He picked up a watch and asked, "Surely not this watch, Grandma?"

"Yes, it was your Grandfather Beverley's," she said. "I know he'd want you to have his gold watch."

David fondled the watch tenderly. Then he picked up a new pair of pants.

"Long dress pants for Sunday, David," his grandmother said.

David was too stunned to speak. He was so overjoyed that tears came into his eyes.

"I'm so proud to have a grandson like you," she said. "I'm the proudest I've ever been in my life. You have brought me joy and happiness I have never known before."

Then Grandma Beverley walked closer to David.

"Bend down," she said, "so I can hug and kiss you. You're taller than I am now. You're the beatinest boy that ever grew up in this valley!"

There was a new light in Grandma Beverley's eyes, and in David's, too, as they looked at each other on this white Christmas morning.

Author's Original Note

I hope you have enjoyed this story about David and his Grandma Beverley because I knew just such a boy very well and I have eaten many good meals cooked by his grandmother, using this very luncheon set of the story. I remember the first meal I ate from this luncheon set. I said, "I never saw a prettier tablecloth, or prettier napkins." And Grandma smiled. "These didn't come from a store," she said. "They are made from feed sacks and they are one of the nicest Christmas presents I ever got." Then she told me the story I have written for you.

Making pretty and useful things out of feed sacks is an old story to most of the 4-H boys and girls and the FFA's (Future Farmers of America), and to all the people in the areas where feed sacks are used. My wife's father, Emmett Norris, was manager of a feed store in Greenup, Kentucky. I used to go there and buy feed for my chickens and for the birds that build nests around our house. And often I'd see a farmer, after his wife had made her selection, buy as many as ten sacks of the same color and design. I knew his wife was probably going to make window curtains or quilts or clothes for the children.

One of the most attractive sights I ever saw was a little shack down in a gap between two high hills. I walked past it one day in late September when I was going to Little Sandy River to fish. The weather had turned the planks almost as brown as an autumn leaf, and the large oaks around the house had scattered leaves over the yard. And the window curtains were made out of feed sacks in the autumn-leaf design, just like David's.

Another time I was visiting friends in a house just outside a city. They took me on a tour all over the house. When they got to their eleven- year-old daughter's room, I was amazed at how attractive it was. Then they told me that all by herself she had made the curtains, the quilt, and the dressing-table skirt — all out of feed sacks.

Grandma and David and Mrs. Byrd may not have been the first in this country to use feed-sack tablecloths and napkins. But Mrs. Byrd was the first one I knew to do it. And when she, a smart woman with good taste, saw what could be done with feed sacks, other people followed her example. It isn't any wonder, then, is it, that the feed-sack companies hire artists to design the sacks and that each company tries to get the most attractive designs that will be made into ladies' aprons, babies' rompers, boys' shirts, girls' dresses, pajamas, and lots of other beautiful things?

Jesse Stuart

About The Author

Jesse Stuart (1906-1984) was one of America's best-known and best-loved writers. During his lifetime he published more than 2,000 poems, 460 short stories, and nine novels. His more than 60 published books include biography, autobiography, essays, and juvenile works as well as poetry and fiction. These books have immortalized his native hill country.

Stuart also taught and lectured extensively. His teaching experience ranged from the one-room schoolhouses of his youth in Eastern Kentucky to the American University in Cairo, Egypt, and embraced years of service as school superintendent, high school teacher, and high school principal. "First, last, always," said Jesse Stuart, "I am a teacher. . . . Good teaching is forever, and the teacher is immortal."

Stuart wrote eight books for young people. The Jesse Stuart Foundation, a non-profit organization devoted to preserving the legacy of Jesse Stuart, is making these books available to a new generation of readers. *A Penny's Worth Of Character, Hie To The Hunters, A Jesse Stuart Reader,* and *A Ride With Huey The Engineer* have recently been re-issued. *The Beatinest Boy* will be followed by a biography of Jesse Stuart for young readers.

Illustrated by Robert Henneberger, a graduate of the Rhode Island School of Design. Book and cover design by Rocky Zornes, ZAK Productions, Lexington, Kentucky.

Junior Books By Jesse Stuart

Andy Finds a Way $6 softback/$12 hardback

The Beatinest Boy $5 softback/$10 hardback

Old Ben $3 softback/$10 hardback

A Penny's Worth of Character $3 softback/$10 hardback

Red Mule $6 softback/$12 hardback

A Ride With Huey The Engineer $6 softback/$12 hardback

The Rightful Owner $6 softback/$12 hardback

Mail your order to:

The Jesse Stuart Foundation
P.O. Box 391
Ashland, KY 41114
(606) 329-5233

School Discount

While supplies last, the JSF offers classroom sets of 30 or more books at a 40 percent discount.

NEW TEACHER'S GUIDE

Winners is a unique teacher's guide designed to accompany junior books by Jesse Stuart. It contains work sheets designed to enhance and build self-esteem and provide values education. Written by Dr. Jean Wilson Houck and Deborah Hamm-Schwartz, Winners is a valuable resource for teachers in grades three through six who wish to update and enrich their reading programs. It is designed to be used with: The Rightful Owner, A Ride With Huey the Engineer, Old Ben, The Beatinest Boy, A Penny's Worth of Character and Andy Finds A Way.

These books are marvelous stories of children in rural America. They capture the imagination of children everywhere. For rural children, the stories are about surroundings which are familiar and subjects which are relevant to their lives. The stories and language arts activists will encourage pride in the children's culture and in themselves. The self-concept activities will reinforce both their view of personal worth and traditional American values.

The 141-page teacher's workbook comes in a three-ring binder for ease in copying work sheets for classroom use. It is a must for every teacher who uses Stuart's junior books.

Send $27.50 per copy, plus $2 for shipping and handling to:

The Jesse Stuart Foundation
P.O. Box 391
Ashland, KY 41114
(606) 329-5233